EALRIS
13140005134209

Katie Morag and the Tiresome Ted

D0230772

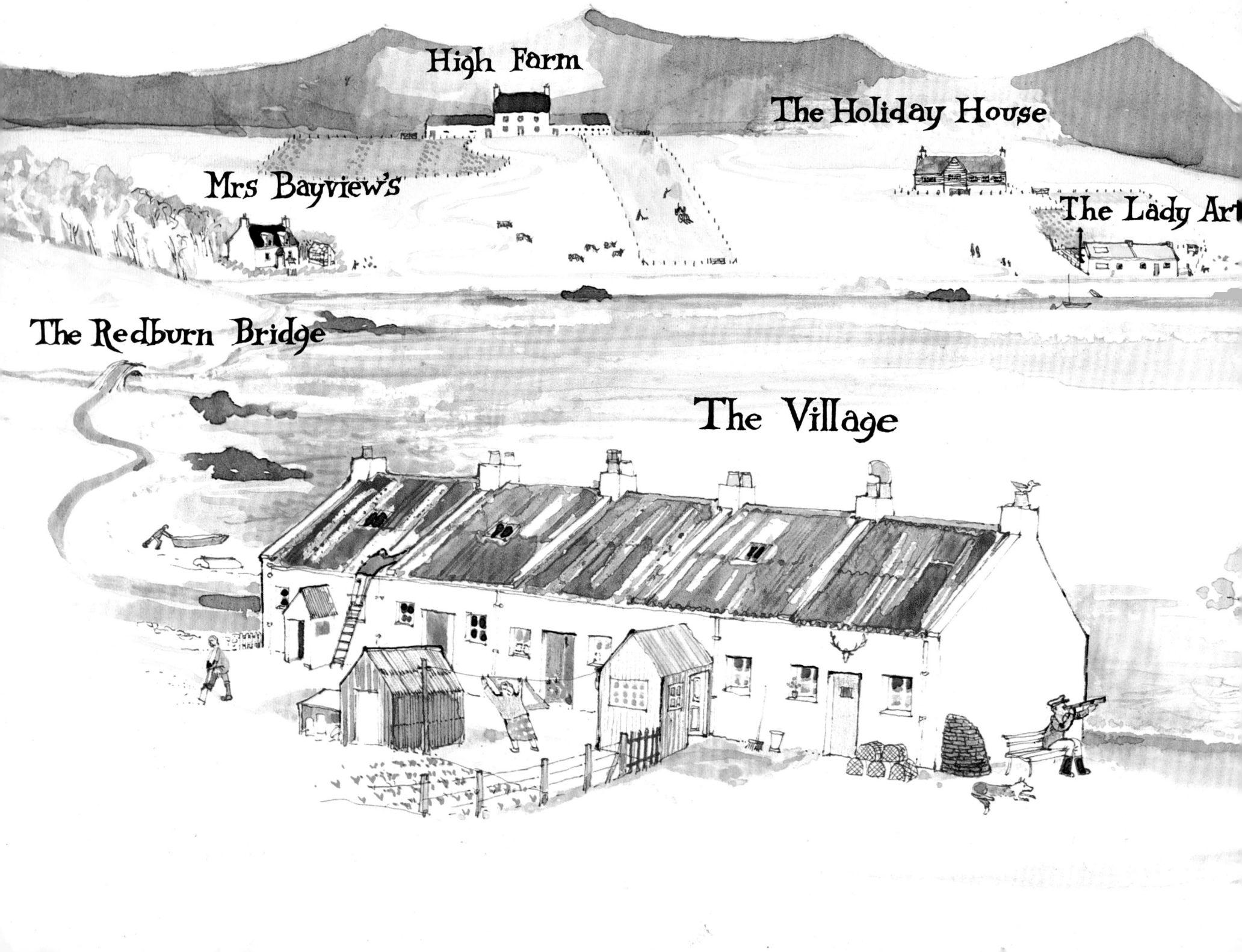
High Farm
The Holiday House
Mrs Bayview's
The Lady Art
The Redburn Bridge
The Village

THE ISLE of STRUAY

KATIE MORAG AND THE TIRESOME TED
A RED FOX BOOK 978 1 849 41095 3

First published in Great Britain by The Bodley Head, an imprint of
Random House Children's Publishers UK A Random House Group Company

Bodley Head edition published 1986
Red Fox edition published 1999
This Red Fox edition published 2010

5 7 9 10 8 6

Copyright © Mairi Hedderwick 1986

The right of Mairi Hedderwick to be identified as the author and illustrator of this work
has been asserted in accordance with the Copyright, Designs and Patents Act 1988.

All rights reserved

Red Fox Books are published by Random House Children's Publishers UK,
61-63 Uxbridge Road, London W5 5SA

www.randomhousechildrens.co.uk
www.**randomhouse**.co.uk

Addresses for companies within The Random House Group Limited can be found at:
www.**randomhouse**.co.uk/offices.htm

THE RANDOM HOUSE GROUP Limited Reg. No. 954009

A CIP catalogue record for this book is available from the British Library

Printed in Italy

The Random House Group Limited supports The Forest Stewardship Council® (FSC®), the leading
international forest-certification organisation. Our books carrying the FSC label are printed on FSC®-certified paper.
FSC is the only forest-certification scheme supported by the leading environmental organisations, including Greenpeace.
Our paper procurement policy can be found at www.randomhouse.co.uk/environment.

Katie Morag and the Tiresome Ted

Mairi Hedderwick

EAST AYRSHIRE LEISURE TRUST	
513420	
Bertrams	07/01/2015
	£6.99

RED FOX

There was great excitement on the Isle of Struay. Mrs McColl at the Post Office had had a new baby, and everyone was delighted.

Everyone, that is, except Katie Morag. She had been in a bad mood ever since the new baby had arrived.

"No one talks to *me* any more," she grumbled to herself, "or brings *me* presents."

"Don't worry," everyone said knowingly. "Katie Morag will soon get over it."

But Katie Morag could not and would not get over it. She kept doing naughty things, like stamping her feet and nipping her little brother, Liam.

One day she was so cross that she stomped all the way down to the jetty and kicked her friendly old one-eyed teddy bear into the sea.

"Tiresome Ted!" she shouted, as he disappeared into the choppy waves.

Mrs McColl was at her wit's end. "How can I cope with running the Post Office *and* with looking after the new baby *and* Liam, when Katie Morag is behaving like this?" she asked, throwing her arms up in despair.

Mr McColl said that he *was* trying to help.

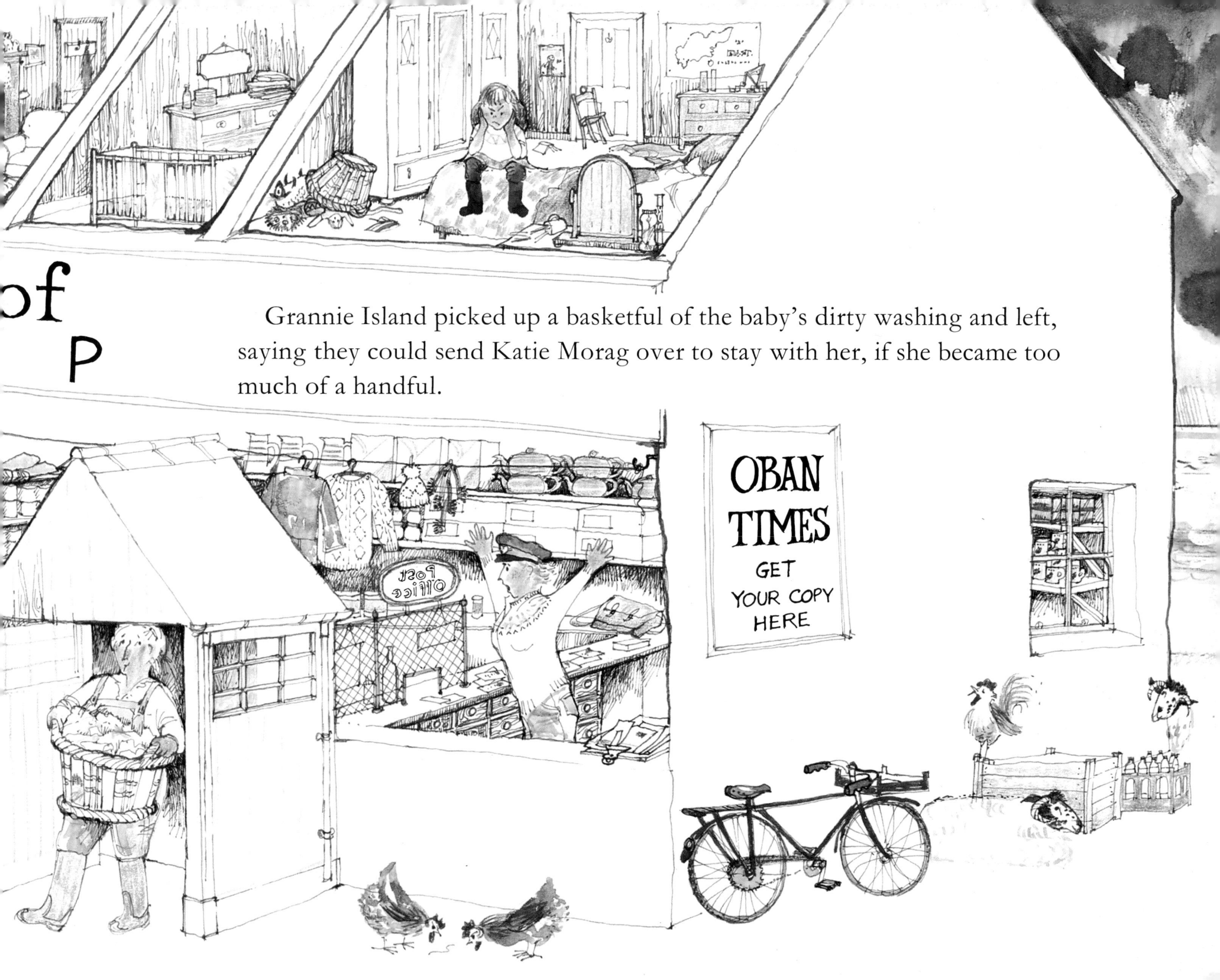

of
P

Grannie Island picked up a basketful of the baby's dirty washing and left, saying they could send Katie Morag over to stay with her, if she became too much of a handful.

That night the first of the winter storms battered at the window. Katie Morag could not sleep. She wondered what had become of her old teddy and she began to wish she hadn't thrown him away.

She crept over to Liam's bed and took his hot-water bottle . . . but it didn't make her feel much better.

NOVEMBER
M T W T F S S

The next morning things seemed even worse. Katie Morag woke up to a wet bed. Liam thought it was very funny, but Mrs McColl was furious. It was the last straw.

"I think perhaps Katie Morag should go to Grannie Island's for a few days, after all," sighed Mr McColl.

Katie Morag trudged slowly over to Grannie Island's on the other side of the Bay.

"Having bad moods is very tiring," she thought to herself, and so engrossed was she with her own crossness that she didn't notice a familiar object being flung up by the waves of the incoming tide.

The bad weather lasted for two whole days and nights. Grannie Island could not get on with the washing, and Katie Morag was forced to stay indoors. She wondered how everyone was back at home.

And all the while her old teddy bear lay abandoned on the beach in front of Grannie Island's house. He was a sorry sight.

At last, the rain stopped and the sun came out. Katie Morag felt much better and she decided to stop being in a bad mood. She went down to the high tide-line to collect driftwood for Grannie's stove.

Katie Morag found all sorts of other interesting things that had been washed up by the storm: a ball for Liam, a box for Mr McColl, a bottle for Mrs McColl and a beautiful, big conch shell.

"I'll give this to the new baby," thought Katie Morag, "and show her how to hear the sea."

ALICE OBE

It was only then that Katie Morag noticed the two furry arms sticking up through the seaweed. She couldn't believe her eyes. Old Ted wasn't lost, after all.

Katie Morag rushed back to Grannie's and dried her teddy out by the stove. She filled his tummy with some fluffy sheep's wool and then laboriously began sewing up the large tear in his tummy.

But even with his new eye on, he still looked the worse for the wear. When Grannie Island wasn't looking, Katie Morag took something out of the washing-basket.

The journey back to the Post Office seemed to take ages. Katie Morag couldn't wait to get home to show everyone the things she had found down by the shore.

The other islanders were pleased to see Katie Morag looking like her old self again. "She's got over it," they all said, nodding their heads.

"Thank you for the lovely presents, Katie Morag," said Mrs McColl. "And thank you, Grannie Island, for doing all that washing."

"It's good to have our Katie Morag back, and to see Old Ted again," said Mr McColl, smiling.

"I'll never, ever throw him away again, or call him Tiresome Ted," said Katie Morag, and she meant it.

And nobody said a thing about the missing Babygro from Mrs McColl's washing-basket, which was perhaps just as well.

ISLE of STRUAY
SHOP & POST OFFICE
OBAN
TIMES
GET
YOUR COPY
HERE

Join Katie Morag on more adventures!

Katie Morag and the Big Boy Cousins
Katie Morag Delivers the Mail
Katie Morag and the Riddles
Katie Morag and the Wedding
Katie Morag and the Birthdays
Katie Morag and the Dancing Class
Katie Morag and the Two Grandmothers
Katie Morag and the Grand Concert
Katie Morag and the New Pier
Katie Morag's Island Stories
More Katie Morag Island Stories
The Big Katie Morag Storybook
The Second Katie Morag Storybook